The 300 Pound Cat

The 300 Pound Cat

By Rosamond Dauer
Illustrations by Skip Morrow

A Snuggle & Read Story Book

AN AVON CAMELOT BOOK

For Louise Welleck
—R. D.
For Brie Elizabeth Sprenger
—S. M.

3rd grade reading level has been determined by using the Fry Readability Scale.

AVON BOOKS
A division of
The Hearst Corporation
959 Eighth Avenue
New York, New York 10019

The Holt, Rinehart and Winston edition contains the following
Library of Congress Cataloging in Publication Data:

Dauer, Rosamond.
   The 300 pound cat.
   Summary: William Cat's taste for typewriters and
boots alarms his parents and doctor.
   [1. Diet—Fiction 2. Cats—Fiction] I.Morrow, Skip. II. Title.
PZ7.D2615Aab   [E]   81-1924   AACR2

First Camelot Printing, April, 1983

CAMELOT TRADEMARK REG. U.S. PAT. OFF. AND IN
OTHER COUNTRIES, MARCA REGISTRADA, HECHO EN
U.S.A.

Printed in the U.S.A.

BAN   10   9   8   7   6   5   4   3   2   1

When William Cat was born
he was quite small.

Mother Cat fixed
peas and potatoes for him
and took William for walks
in a cat carriage.

Father Cat sang songs
and started a bird stamp
collection for him.

After a while,
William Cat was not happy
eating peas and potatoes.

He was, in fact,
growing out and up.

One weekend,
he took a fancy
to turnips.

"Turnips!"
exclaimed Mother Cat.
"What a funny vegetable!"
But she cooked them for William.

"More turnips, please,"
said William.

Soon, he looked a little bit
like a turnip.

"I'm worried,"
Father Cat said.

The next week
William decided he liked typewriters, too.

"Typewriters!" cried Father Cat.
"How outlandish!"
But he bought used typewriters for William to eat.

"More typewriters, please,"
said William.

William gained weight.
He was eating peas, potatoes,
turnips, and typewriters.

After a while, he looked
a little like a typewriter.

He started to make noises.
He went Tap! Tap! Tap!
Every once in a while
he sounded like a small bell.
DING!

The next week
William was hungry again.
He was interested in boots.

"Boots!"
Mother Cat exclaimed.
"You look disgusting
with those laces hanging out
of your mouth!"

"More boots, please,"
said William.

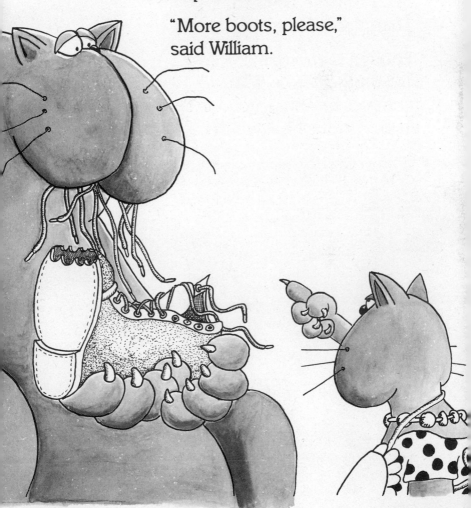

And William ate boots, peas and potatoes,
turnips and typewriters. He was very big indeed.

Father Cat bought the largest cat scale
he could find and weighed William.

"300 pounds!" he cried.
"That's too much!"

"Enough is enough!"
said Mother Cat to William,
who was beginning to look like
an enormous boot when he sat down.

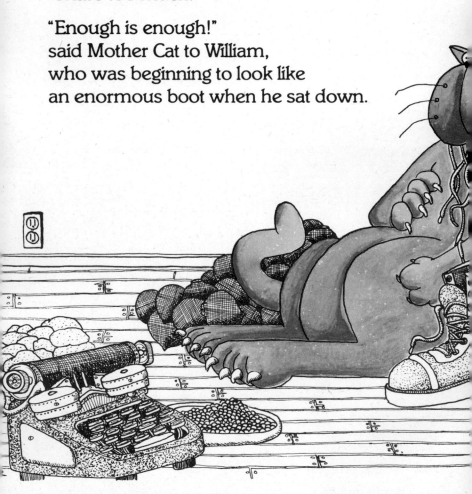

Mother and Father Cat
took William
to the family doctor.

Dr. Cat took one look at William
and said, "My goodness!"

Then he took a big ladder,
climbed up,
and looked down William's throat.
"Ugh!" he said.

He then listened to William's heart,
and asked him
to stick out his tongue.

When he was through,
Dr. Cat said, "Ah-hem!
I don't know why,
but William seems healthy.
However, he should
go on a diet."

"A diet!" cried William.
"How cruel!"

"No more turnips,"
said Father Cat.

"No more typewriters,"
said Mother Cat.

"No more boots,"
said Dr. Cat.

"Rats!"
said William to Dr. Cat.
"You have not even <u>tasted</u>
a good boot."

"Indeed, I have not,"
Dr. Cat said.

"Here," said William,
"try a tiny bite."

"YUMMY!" Dr. Cat exclaimed.

"And here, Mother,
try a bite of turnip."

"Oh terrific!"
Mother Cat said in surprise.

"And Father,"
William Cat said,
"here are the letters
I, F, and **X**
from a very small typewriter."

"Golly! This is good!"
cried Father Cat.

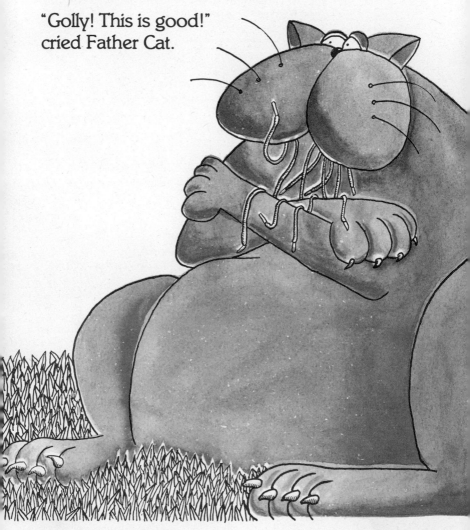

"Even so," William said,
"I will go on a diet
because I can't get into
my room or the house."

Soon, there were four
VERY LARGE CATS
in the town.

They weighed 75 pounds each, which showed that they all watched their weight.

Sometimes Mother and Father Cat went Tap! Tap! Tap!

Sometimes Dr. Cat went DING!

Sometimes William looked like a turnip again.

Once
they all looked like boots
at the same time.
But they did not let boot laces
hang out of their mouths.

In large measure,
they were very happy
and stood out in a crowd—

especially William,
who was taller.